WHERE HOPE TOOK ROOT

Grace Multiplied

Blessed Beyond Measure

A Short Story

Dr. Arnette West

Published by JATNE Publishing, LLC

ISBN: 978-1-958117-38-5 (paperback)
ISBN: 978-1-958117-39-2 (eBook)

Library of Congress Control Number: 2026900367

This is a work of fiction. All events and characters in this story are solely the product of the author's imagination. Any similarities between any characters and situations presented in this story to any individuals living or dead or actual places and situations are pure coincidence.

Printed in the USA

JATNE Publishing, LLC
Sumter, SC

DEDICATION

To those learning to carry the blessings
they once prayed for…

To the hearts stretched by joy, responsibility,
and the unexpected weight of abundance—

May you remember that grace is here too.

In every sigh,
in every sunrise,
in every ordinary moment of love—

Your strength is your steady place.

You are not overwhelmed.
You are held.
You are seen.
You are supported.

You are carried by a God whose
strength fills every gap.

May this story remind you that blessing is not
always tidy, grace is not always quiet, and
miracles do not always come gently.

FOR READERS, LEADERS & BOOK DISCUSSION GROUPS

If you would like to use *Where Hope Took Root* beyond reading, there is a list of questions and prayer at the end.

If you will lead a book club or group study, additional resources are available to enhance your experience. These include **Faith & Life Application** questions to deepen personal reflection and a **Facilitator's Resource List** with recommended books, devotionals, and discussion tools. To request these materials, please reach out through jatnepublishing.org.

Table of Contents

INTRODUCTION

WHEN GRACE MULTIPLIES

There is a moment after prayer is answered when faith must learn a new language. For Naomi, that moment came quietly—not with fanfare or certainty, but with the gentle realization that life had moved forward. The waiting she once knew so well had given way to fullness. The ache that shaped her prayers no longer defined her days. What she had once longed for was now present, tangible, and alive.

Hope had taken root.

But as Naomi would soon discover, answered prayers introduce new questions. Faith that once survived on trust alone must now learn how to walk responsibly in abundance. Grace, when it arrives, does not simply comfort, it calls.

This book begins in that sacred in-between place.

Where gratitude meets responsibility.

Where blessing meets stewardship.

Where faith must mature beyond survival.

Grace Multiplied is not the story of arrival—it is the story of adjustment. It explores what happens when God gives more than we imagined and invites us to grow into the capacity to carry it. Naomi and Christopher learn that grace is not passive; it is active, shaping decisions, deepening humility, and refining trust.

As blessings multiply, so do opportunities for growth. Joy expands, but so does vulnerability. Faith is tested not by lack, but by abundance. Through new responsibilities, unexpected pressures, and moments that require discernment, Naomi learns grace must be stewarded as carefully as hope was once guarded.

This is the season where God teaches His children not just how to receive, but how to remain rooted.

Grace multiplies in forgiveness practiced daily. It multiplies in unity protected intentionally. It multiplies when gratitude turns into obedience.

If *Where Hope Took Root* was a story for those still waiting, *Grace Multiplied* is a companion for those learning how to live faithfully once the waiting ends. It reminds us that God's generosity is never careless and every blessing carries an invitation to grow deeper, walk wiser, and trust God beyond the miracle.

This book invites you to reflect on your own seasons of abundance. To consider how grace has shown up in your life—not just in what you have received, but in who you are becoming. Because what God plants in hope, He multiplies through grace, and He does so with purpose.

Part I:

When Grace Arrives

When God's answer exceeds
what you imagined.

Chapter One

The Unexpected Call

The phone rang late that afternoon—the kind of ring that slices through the ordinary and rearranges everything you thought you knew. Naomi almost didn't answer. She was stirring a pot of soup, humming softly, her mind wandering through the familiar rhythm of waiting—waiting for news, waiting for direction, waiting for the next chapter that God had yet to unfold.

"Mrs. Matthews?" The voice on the other end was gentle but carried a weight that made her heart quicken. "This is Mariah from the agency. We have some news."

Naomi froze, spoon mid-air, eyes darting toward the living room where Christopher was reading. He looked up instantly, sensing the shift in her tone.

"Yes…Yes, I'm here," she managed, her voice trembling.

Mariah continued, "We've matched you and your husband with a mother who has chosen you both. She's due…sooner than expected. And, well…it's triplets."

The word echoed—*triplets*.

For a moment, Naomi thought she had misheard. She pressed the phone tighter to her ear, her knees growing weak.

"Did you say three?"

"Yes, ma'am. Three beautiful babies. Two girls and one boy. All healthy so far. The mother wants them to stay together and she felt peace when she saw your profile."

Naomi's free hand covered her mouth as tears welled up. She turned toward Christopher, eyes wide with a mixture of disbelief and awe.

"Three," she whispered.

He stood up slowly, the words sinking in like sunlight breaking through morning fog. *Three.* The number rolled through his mind—the Father, the Son, and the Holy Spirit. The divine trinity. A symbol of wholeness.

He reached for Naomi's hand, steady and warm. "God really does think differently than we do," he said softly, a smile breaking through his stunned expression.

That night, neither of them slept. They lay awake talking about cribs, diapers, names, and nursery colors. And about how their faith had been stretched in the waiting, only to be expanded in the blessing.

Yet, underneath the excitement, a quiet question pulsed in Naomi's heart: *Can I handle more than I prayed for?* She remembered the countless nights she had prayed for one child—one heartbeat to call her own. Never had she dared to ask for three. Was she ready for such a blessing, such a responsibility?

As she watched the moonlight pour across their bedroom wall, she felt God whisper the same truth He had spoken long ago through the prophet Isaiah: *"My thoughts are higher than your thoughts."* It wasn't about what she could handle. It was about what He could do through her.

In the days that followed, Naomi and Christopher moved with purpose and awe. They prepared a nursery that could hold not only three babies, but the fullness of God's promise. Family and friends offered help, donations poured in, and every step reminded them that grace had already gone ahead of them.

Naomi often found herself standing in the middle of the nursery, hand resting on the edge of a tiny crib, whispering prayers of gratitude. The room smelled of new paint and lavender—the scent of beginnings. She still felt nervous, still unsure, but faith anchored her.

"Lord," she prayed one evening, "You didn't just answer our prayer; You multiplied it. Help me to walk in this blessing with peace and purpose. Teach me to trust Your strength when mine runs out."

And in that quiet moment, she felt it—the steady assurance that the same God who had called them to this moment would carry them through every sleepless night and every new sunrise ahead.

God's blessings often exceed our imagination. His timing doesn't always align with our expectations, but His purpose is always. As Naomi drifted to sleep, her last thought lingered softly in the air: *"Can I handle more than I prayed for?"*

And Heaven whispered back, *"You won't have to handle it alone."*

Chapter Two

Overflowing Emotions

The first few weeks after bringing the babies home felt like stepping into a whirlwind. Diapers overflowed faster than Naomi could fold the laundry. The washing machine sang without ceasing, and the scent of baby powder mingled with coffee and desperation. On brave nights, when all three tiny voices decided to cry in harmony, Naomi joked they could record a worship chorus called *"Lord, Help Us Now."*

Morning sunlight poured through the blinds, illuminating a living room that looked more like a nursery supply aisle than a home. Bottles lined the kitchen counter like little soldiers ready for battle. Burp cloths draped over the arms of chairs and pacifiers nestled beneath the couch cushions.

She stood in the middle of it all, holding baby number two while baby number three wailed in protest from the bassinet. Somewhere in the background, the coffee maker gurgled its final breath—*again*.

She smiled weakly and muttered, "Your grace is sufficient, Lord…but caffeine would sure help."

When Naomi first envisioned motherhood, she pictured tidy mornings, soft lullabies, and matching onesies neatly folded in drawers. However, reality came dressed in mismatched socks and spit-up-stained T-shirts. The once-serene, organized woman now embraced a simple mantra: "Clean-ish is good enough."

Christopher wasn't faring much better. He maintained a spreadsheet to keep track of which baby he had fed last, given his full-time job, helping at church, and late-night diaper runs. He'd even tried labeling bottles with initials—*A, B, and C*—but that quickly fell apart the day he accidentally gave "Baby C" her sister's milk and got a look from Naomi that said everything without a single word.

By the third week, both parents had given up on schedules and learned the art of grace-filled improvisation. Some mornings began at 3 a.m.; others never really ended. Yet, in the middle of the exhaustion, something beautiful was happening.

One evening, Naomi sat rocking one baby, her eyes heavy but her spirit alert. She whispered, "Lord, I'm trying so hard to get it right."

In the stillness, she felt a gentle nudge in her heart: *You don't have to get it right. You just have to be here.*

That truth broke something open inside her. Much time had passed since she had measured her worth by her ability to hold it all together. But now, surrounded by tiny cries and half-folded laundry, she realized that perfection wasn't the goal; *presence* was. Grace wasn't about getting ahead of the chaos; it was about letting God meet her in the middle of it.

A few days later, Christopher came home to find Naomi sitting on the floor, surrounded by the babies. They sprawled around her like little cherubs in a parade of toys. She laughed—not a polite laugh, but one that came from deep surrender.

"I gave up trying to match their socks," she said between giggles. "They're all wearing polka dots and stripes now. Maybe it's their way of showing individuality."

Christopher dropped his work bag, knelt beside her, and joined in her laughter. "If mismatched socks are the worst thing that happens today," he said, "we're doing great."

They sat there for a while, surrounded by bottle caps, baby wipes, and the unexplainable joy that only comes from letting go. It wasn't the picture-perfect family life they once imagined; it was better. It was *real*.

That night, as the babies finally drifted to sleep and the house settled into rare silence, Naomi sipped reheated coffee. She whispered, "Thank You, Lord, for loving me in the mess."

And deep in her heart, she heard it again—that quiet reassurance: *My grace is sufficient for you. Not your plan, not your performance, just My grace.*

Grace meets us exactly where we are—in the middle of the noise, the mess, and the moments that don't go as planned. It's not about striving for perfection but about resting in God's presence when everything feels imperfect. His grace doesn't demand our strength; it simply invites our surrender.

Later that week, Naomi sent Christopher a photo of three babies lined up in their bouncers, each wearing a different sock, and drooling in unison. The caption read: "Our triplet choir is rehearsing for Sunday. Grace has rhythm—even in chaos."

He replied simply: "Amen to that. And don't forget, your coffee is still in the microwave…again."

CHAPTER THREE

LEARNING TO BREATHE AGAIN

Before motherhood, Naomi lived by structure. Her color-coded planner ruled their household—meal plans in green, prayer times in blue, date nights in red, and *rest days* boldly marked in yellow. Everything once moved to her rhythm. But now, that beloved planner lay buried beneath a heap of burp cloths and unopened mail. She could no longer remember the last time she'd eaten breakfast sitting down or finished a prayer without interruption.

Some mornings, she stood before the mirror, toothbrush in one hand, pacifier in the other, unsure which task came first. The woman who once taught organization seminars now considered brushing her hair a victory.

And yet, beneath the fatigue, her heart held a quiet awe. Life had shifted overnight, and though exhaustion pressed heavily, gratitude still whispered: *You prayed for this.*

When Christopher came home late, smelling of coffee, determination, and long hours, the weight of their new life pressed heavier. He tried to hide it behind a weary grin, but Naomi could see the lines deepening around his eyes. Their conversations usually began with "Did you pick up more formula?" and ended with "Whose turn is it to feed next?"

At the agency, Christopher gave his best. Between ministry meetings, extra shifts, and the pressure of new expenses, he poured himself out daily. Yet the guilt followed him home like a shadow. *You're not doing enough,* it whispered. *You're failing them.*

He wanted to be Naomi's strength, but his own was running low. Some nights, he stood in the nursery doorway just watching—the soft rise and fall of three tiny chests, Naomi humming under her breath—and he'd feel both proud and terrified. He prayed quietly, *Lord, help me lead well, even when I feel lost.*

One particularly long night, after the third attempt to get everyone asleep, Naomi sank into the rocking chair. One baby rested against her chest, their breathing steady and rhythmic. The moonlight spilled through the window, touching bottles, blankets, and an untouched dinner cooling on the table.

"Lord," she whispered, voice trembling, "I'm not enough. I can't do this perfectly."

Her words floated into the silence. She closed her eyes, waiting—half desperate, half expectant. The seconds stretched long enough for tears to fall one by one. Then, something shifted. Not a sound, but a stillness—holy, encompassing. It was as though the air itself leaned closer.

You don't have to be perfect, came the reply, gentle and certain. *You just have to be present.*

The words sank deep, washing over her like warm light. Tears returned, not heavy with frustration this time, but light—cleansing. Scripture rose in her heart like a melody: *My grace is sufficient for you, for My power is made perfect in weakness.*

Naomi exhaled slowly. Grace wasn't a sermon note; it was oxygen. It filled the cracks in her resolve, steadying her heartbeat, anchoring her spirit.

The next morning, she found Christopher pacing the living room—two babies in his arms, a burp cloth slung across his shoulder like a superhero's cape.

"They've been up since four," he said, eyes red but smiling. "I think they're trying to break their own record."

Naomi laughed; a sound she hadn't heard from herself in weeks. "Then we're officially outnumbered."

In that laughter, something healed.

From that day forward, they began to celebrate small victories. When she burned dinner, Naomi laughed instead of crying. When Christopher forgot the wipes again, she teased instead of snapping. They prayed over cold coffee, grateful for five minutes together.

Their home slowly became a sanctuary of imperfect grace. The pressure to perform began to fade. They started noticing holiness hidden in the ordinary—the sacredness of rocking a child at 2 a.m., the miracle of teamwork during diaper duty, the quiet peace of whispering Scripture between yawns.

One evening, while folding tiny onesies, Christopher broke the silence. "I used to think leading meant having all the answers," he said. "But maybe leadership is just…leaning on God when you don't."

Naomi paused, her hands stilling over a soft yellow blanket. "Maybe that's what grace really is," she replied. "God filling in the gaps we can't reach."

They both smiled, the hum of the dryer steady behind them. For the first time in weeks, the quiet didn't feel heavy; it felt hollow.

As months passed, the rhythm of their home softened. The babies began smiling, their laughter echoing through rooms once filled with fatigue. Christopher read short devotionals at breakfast—sometimes managing half a verse before being interrupted by a cry. Naomi filled her journal with raw gratitude:

Today, I chose peace over perfection. The dishes are still in the sink, but the babies are fed and loved. That's enough.

God reminded me He's in the noise, not just the quiet. Grace doesn't wait for calm—it meets me right here, right now.

Naomi once warmed the same bottle three times and never fed it to anyone. Christopher proudly labeled each diaper with initials—only to realize he'd mixed them up all night. Their "date nights" became silent competitions to see who could fall asleep first. Once, Naomi accidentally texted their grocery list to the pastor, who replied, "Praying for milk and grace in abundance." Those moments became lifelines—proof that even laughter could be worship.

Grace met them in every messy corner. It covered the spilled milk, the weary sighs, the imperfect attempts. It whispered that God's presence mattered more than their performance. His strength didn't demand control; it blossomed through surrender.

Each day, they learned anew that family life wasn't about holding everything together. It was about trusting the One who held them.

Late one night, Naomi wrote in her journal:

Perfection was the idol I didn't know I worshiped. But grace—grace is the melody that brings peace to the noise. Every cry, every spill, every sleepless night is its own hymn of surrender. And somehow, in this holy chaos, I am learning to rest.

She closed the journal, the lamp casting a soft glow across the three cribs aligned like a tiny choir.

"Father, Son, and Holy Spirit," she whispered with a smile.

The babies stirred, each turning in rhythm as if answering her prayer. Naomi brushed her thumb over the edge of the journal, heart full. Tomorrow, they would learn again how to see God reflected in every face, every sound, and every moment of grace multiplied.

Part II:

When Grace Stretches You

Learning to love, lead,
and lean on God in the press.

Chapter Four

Trinity in the Crib

Naomi stood at the doorway of the nursery just before dawn. The soft glow from the night-light bathed the room in gold, casting gentle halos around the three tiny cribs lined up side by side. Each baby stirred at different rhythms—one cooed, one sighed, one flung a hand in the air as if praising unseen angels.

She smiled through sleepy eyes. *Three little miracles,* she thought. *Three reflections of the same love.*

It had been months since that chaotic first night when she thought she couldn't do it all. Now, the house still hummed with noise, but it was a different kind of sound—one that felt like music. Laughter mixed with lullabies, and in the ordinary rhythm of feeding, bathing, and praying, Naomi had found a new kind of worship.

Christopher appeared beside her, his voice a quiet hum. "They're starting to look like each other more every day," he whispered. "Sometimes, I can't tell who's who until they smile."

Naomi leaned her head against his shoulder. "And yet, each one is so different. Peace, compassion, boldness." She pointed to each crib in turn. "It's strange—I see parts of God in them."

Christopher nodded slowly. "Like the Trinity," he said. "Different, but one."

They stood there for a while, just listening—the steady rhythm of breathing, the quiet miracle of life multiplied by three. The thought sank deep into both their hearts. Their home had become a living illustration of divine unity: one family, many hearts, joined by the same Spirit.

Later that morning, sunlight spilled across the kitchen floor. Naomi poured two mugs of coffee and sat at the table, her Bible open to Matthew 28:19. Her eyes fell on the words, *"In the name of the Father, and of the Son, and of the Holy Spirit."*

She underlined the verse slowly, thinking of the night before—their whispered observation about the babies, how God's nature was somehow reflected in their tiny personalities. It wasn't theology to her now; it was life, moving and breathing before her eyes.

One baby, whom they'd nicknamed "Peace," rarely cried. He slept soundly and smiled easily. He reminded her of the Father's steadiness—constant, safe, dependable. The second, "Compassion," had the softest gaze, as if she could feel everyone's needs before they were spoken. Naomi often thought of Jesus when she held her—tender, healing, always reaching. The third, "Boldness," was already loud and fearless, a whirlwind of energy who refused to stay still. That one, Naomi decided, carried the spark of the Holy Spirit—untamed, powerful, always moving.

She laughed softly to herself. *Only God could hide His fingerprints in three different hearts and call it family.*

That Sunday, they decided it was time.

"Let's dedicate them," Christopher said as he buttoned his shirt, balancing one baby on his knee. "We've been blessed beyond what we asked for. It's time to give them back to the One who gave them to us."

The church watched Naomi and Christopher's story unfold from the beginning—the waiting, the heartbreak, the miracle calls from the agency. So, when the couple walked in that morning carrying three bundled blessings, the congregation erupted in tears and applause.

Pastor Henry's voice trembled as he spoke. "We watched you sow in tears," he said gently, "and now you're reaping in joy. These children are not just your blessing—they are God's testimony."

Naomi's heart swelled as she and Christopher stood before the altar, surrounded by family, friends, and the village that had prayed them through. When the pastor lifted each baby and anointed them with oil, he spoke softly but firmly:

"Father, may this child grow in Your peace."

"Son, may this one carry Your compassion."

"Holy Spirit, may this one walk in Your power."

Each declaration echoed like music through the sanctuary. The moment felt sacred; like Heaven itself leaned close to listen. Naomi wept, but her tears were not from exhaustion or fear this time. They were tears of recognition. That evening, after the last visitor had gone and the babies were finally asleep, Naomi sat on the edge of the bed, the dedication certificates resting in her lap.

"I feel like we witnessed something holy today," she said quietly.

Christopher turned off the lamp and slid beside her. "We did," he replied. "We've seen God's promise multiplied. They're reminders that He doesn't just answer prayers; He exceeds them."

Naomi nodded, eyes glistening. "It's like each of them carries a piece of Heaven home."

She opened *purpose in love.* Purpose is never discovered through ambition alone. It is revealed through alignment. When she loved—without agenda, without proof, without guarantee—she aligned herself with the very nature of God. And because God is love, purpose was already waiting on the other side of obedience.

In the weeks that followed, the symbolism of the Trinity seemed to weave itself into everything. When one baby cried, another laughed. When one slept, another watched. And somehow, it all balanced. There was order in the movement, harmony in the difference—an unspoken rhythm that reminded Naomi of divine orchestration.

Sometimes, late at night, she and Christopher would pray together over the cribs. "Lord," he'd whisper, "teach us to love like You—selflessly, patiently, without fear."

And Naomi would add softly, "Let our home mirror Your presence. Let these children see You in us."

Life didn't suddenly become easy. There were still diaper explosions, long nights, and coffee reheated three times. But grace had changed the way they saw it all. What used to feel like chaos now felt like worship.

Each smile was a hymn. Each giggle was a verse. Each sleepless night was a lesson in endurance and love.

She grabbed her journal and began to write:

Today, we offered back to God what He first gave us. I see now that every answered prayer carries responsibility—to nurture, to teach, to reflect His love. These three aren't just our children. They are a living parable: Father, Son, and Spirit—unity in diversity, strength in surrender.

Sometimes, as she rocked one baby while the others slept, Naomi would whisper, "You belong to Him." The words weren't a ritual. They were her reminder that motherhood itself was ministry, and every diaper change, every lullaby, every whispered prayer was sacred work.

One afternoon, while Christopher worked in the garden, Naomi stood at the window watching him. The flowers they'd once planted "where hope took root" were in full bloom again. She could almost hear the echo of their story—the long wait, the tears, the moment of surrender, and now, the abundance.

This is what grace looks like, she thought. *It grows when you least expect it, multiplies when you think you've run out, and blossoms in places you thought were barren.*

As evening settled, Naomi peeked once more into the nursery. Peace, Compassion, and Boldness slept soundly, side by side, their tiny breaths rising and falling in rhythm.

She whispered a prayer over them, "Father, thank You for teaching us through these little ones. For showing us Your steadiness, Your tenderness, Your fire. May our home always echo Heaven."

The room grew still again and she felt the same presence she'd known that first weary night—the same whisper of grace, the same promise of strength.

Christopher joined her, slipping his arm around her shoulders. "You know," he said softly, "I think we just met the Trinity—one smile at a time."

Naomi smiled back. "And to think," she whispered, "it all started with a yes we were afraid to give."

They stood together in the quiet, watching over the cribs—their faith, their promise, their miracle multiplied.

Chapter Five

When Love Feels Thin

The triplets were six months old when Naomi first noticed the quiet distance between her and Christopher. It wasn't loud or obvious—no shouting, no slammed doors—just a subtle thinning, like the air between them had grown heavy.

The babies were thriving, full of personality and motion. Days began before sunrise and blurred into nights filled with soft cries and bottle feedings. There was joy, yes, but it was buried under exhaustion. Naomi and Christopher were surviving, not connecting.

He still kissed her goodbye each morning, but the gesture felt mechanical. She still prayed for him each night, but sometimes her prayers ended in frustration rather than gratitude.

One evening, as she rocked Peace to sleep, she glanced at the clock—10:47 p.m. Christopher still wasn't home. The house was dim except for the lamp near the crib. The rhythmic sound of the rocking chair matched the faint ticking of the clock on the wall. *Tick. Rock. Tick. Rock.*

When the front door finally opened, Christopher moved quietly, dropping his bag near the entryway. He looked at her from across the room, eyes weary but kind.

"Hey," he said softly.

"Hey," she answered, her voice carrying both relief and resentment.

He rubbed the back of his neck. "Sorry I'm late. I had to meet with a client who's been dragging his feet on a project. Then the church board called—"

Naomi stopped rocking. "You don't have to explain," she said, a little too quickly.

But the silence that followed was thick. Both knew it wasn't about work or ministry. It was about the growing space between them—the unspoken question of whether their love could still breathe beneath the weight of responsibility.

The next few weeks passed in a rhythm that neither wanted but both endured. Their conversations revolved around feedings, bills, and schedules. When Christopher prayed at dinner, his words were short. When Naomi smiled, it rarely reached her eyes.

One Sunday morning, as they prepared for church, the tension finally cracked. Christopher stood in the kitchen, holding a baby bottle and searching for words.

"Naomi," he began, "we can't keep going like this. We're both here, but not really *here*."

She didn't look up from the diaper bag she was packing. "I know," she said flatly. "But I don't know how to fix it."

Christopher sighed. "Maybe we don't have to fix it. Maybe we just need to *feel* it—talk about it, instead of pretending it's fine."

Her hands froze over the bag. She wanted to argue, to say she didn't have time to "feel" anything. But deep down, she knew he was right. Love wasn't supposed to disappear under laundry and lists—it was meant to be fought for.

That afternoon, Naomi slipped away while the babies napped and sat outside near the garden—the place where hope had once taken root. The flowers were overgrown now, wild and unruly, yet beautiful in their persistence. She ran her fingers through the soil and whispered, "Lord, what happened to us?"

The breeze carried no answer, only the rustling of leaves and the faint hum of creation. Then a Scripture surfaced in her spirit: *"Let us not become weary in doing good, for at the proper time we will reap a harvest if we do not give up."*

She closed her eyes. *Don't give up.* The words stung and soothed all at once.

When Christopher found her there, he didn't speak right away. He sat beside her, knees brushing hers, the silence familiar yet different—gentler, like they were remembering how to breathe the same air.

"Do you remember," he said quietly, "when we used to pray together every night before bed? Not the rushed kind—real prayer?"

Naomi nodded. "I miss that."

"Me too," he admitted. "I think we've both been giving so much for everyone else that we forgot how to give to each other."

She turned to look at him, tears blurring her vision. "I'm scared, Chris. What if this—what if *we* don't feel the same anymore?"

He took her hand, calloused and warm. "Feelings come and go, Naomi. But love—real love—chooses to stay."

That night, for the first time in months, they prayed together—not over bottles or bills, but over their hearts. Christopher led with trembling honesty.

"God, we're tired. We're stretched thin. But You brought us here together for a reason. Remind us how to love like You—patiently, selflessly, without keeping score."

Naomi added softly, "Help us see each other again, Lord. Not just as parents or partners in duty, but as the gift You joined together."

As they prayed, something shifted. It wasn't dramatic or instant. But it was real. The heaviness began to lift, replaced by quiet understanding.

The next morning, the babies woke earlier than usual. Instead of groaning, Christopher chuckled.

"Guess grace starts before sunrise," he said.

Naomi smiled, surprised by how natural it felt.

They began making small changes. Christopher arranged to come home earlier twice a week. Naomi started taking short walks alone to breathe and pray. They carved out one evening each week as "them time"—no talk about diapers or ministry, just laughter and reconnection.

Sometimes, they'd dance in the kitchen to old gospel tunes, careful not to wake the babies. Other nights, they'd read Psalms aloud, taking turns until one of them dozed off mid-verse.

Slowly, warmth returned.

Naomi realized that love didn't grow thinner from hardship—it stretched, and in stretching, it became stronger. The very chaos that had once divided them was now teaching them endurance.

One evening, as the sun dipped low and the babies slept, Christopher pulled Naomi close.

"You know," he said, "I used to pray for a calm life. Now, I just pray for a faithful one."

Naomi rested her head on his chest, feeling the steady rhythm of his heartbeat. "And we're still here," she whispered. "That's faithfulness too."

He smiled. "Love doesn't always feel like fire, Naomi. Sometimes, it's just the quiet flame that refuses to go out."

She closed her eyes and whispered back, "Then let's keep it burning."

That night, Naomi opened her journal and wrote:

Love is not measured by ease or feeling—it's measured by choice. Today, we chose each other again. Even when love feels thin, grace makes it enough.

As she closed the journal, she looked out toward the garden, where moonlight rested on the leaves like soft silver. The flowers swayed gently in the wind, still blooming after all the storms.

She smiled, remembering what the Lord had whispered months ago: *You don't have to be perfect. You just have to be present.*

Presence—that was love's truest form. And as she drifted to sleep beside her husband, Naomi knew they were learning that lesson, one ordinary miracle at a time.

Chapter Six

The Village God Built

The morning sun spilled across the kitchen floor, catching the faint shimmer of cereal dust and baby formula scattered from the night before. Naomi leaned against the counter, sipping her first cup of coffee in what felt like days. The triplets were down for their morning nap—a small miracle in itself—and, for a brief moment, the house exhaled.

She looked around at the toys scattered on the floor, the laundry half-folded on the couch, the stack of unopened mail on the table. It wasn't perfect, but it was real—and it was theirs. Still, even in this peace, Naomi felt the ache of fatigue in her bones.

She whispered a quiet prayer. "Lord, I'm grateful, but I'm tired. I know You said Your grace is sufficient, but today, I could use some backup."

The answer came sooner than she expected.

That afternoon, her friend Denise from church stopped by with a casserole and a smile.

"You don't have to cook tonight," Denise said, waving away Naomi's protests. "Just heat this up and rest those eyes."

Naomi blinked, touched. "Denise, you didn't have to."

"Of course I did," she interrupted. "That's what we do. You took care of everyone else before these babies came. Now, it's our turn."

A few hours later, a text buzzed on Naomi's phone: *Meal train organized. You're covered for the next two weeks.*

Her eyes welled with tears. She hadn't realized how much she needed the help until it showed up at her door.

Over the next few days, meals arrived like manna—soups, salads, casseroles, and fresh bread from women she barely had time to see anymore. One evening, an older church member, Miss Loretta, knocked on the door holding a basket of baby clothes and a soft blanket embroidered with the words *God's Promise*.

"I prayed over every stitch," Miss Loretta said, her eyes crinkling with kindness. "These babies are a testimony, Naomi. Don't let the exhaustion make you forget the miracle."

Naomi hugged her, whispering, "I won't."

Meanwhile, Christopher was finding his own village forming quietly around him. At work, his mentor pulled him aside one afternoon.

"Son," the older man said, "you don't have to carry everything yourself. Delegate, trust your team. Even Moses had Aaron."

Christopher chuckled, realizing how tightly he'd been holding on to control. That evening, as he drove home, he prayed aloud, "Lord, show me how to lead without pride. Teach me to ask for help."

He didn't know it yet, but that prayer would open doors he hadn't considered.

The following Sunday, Pastor Henry called Naomi and Christopher forward during service.

"Church," he said, "we often talk about community, but today we're going to be community. This family has poured into us for years. Now, it's time we pour back."

Within minutes, volunteers signed up for rotating shifts—help with laundry, grocery runs, even babysitting. It wasn't charity; it was covenant.

Naomi tried to protest, but the pastor smiled knowingly.

"You prayed for strength," he said. "Sometimes, strength comes with helping hands."

She laughed through tears. "I see that now."

The weeks that followed were filled with glimpses of God's provision through people. One morning, a neighbor mowed their lawn without asking. Another evening, a group of women gathered in her living room for what was supposed to be a "folding party" but turned into an impromptu worship night as lullabies turned to praise songs.

Christopher found support, too—brothers from the men's ministry who checked in on him, prayed with him, and reminded him that leadership wasn't about perfection but partnership.

"God never meant for us to do life alone," one gentlemen said during their breakfast meeting. "Even Jesus had twelve."

Naomi began journaling again, her words brimming with gratitude:

Today, I learned that community is God's love with skin on. Every meal, every visit, every prayer whispered on our behalf is evidence that we're seen. The village isn't just helping us survive—they're helping us remember that we belong.

As the days went by, their home became a revolving door of grace. Laughter returned, stronger this time. The babies were growing fast—crawling, babbling, and exploring everything in reach. There was still noise, still chaos, but now it was shared.

One Friday evening, the house buzzed with activity. Friends from church gathered for what Naomi jokingly called "Dinner and Diapers." They sang worship songs between bites of casserole and laughed as the babies made their rounds from one set of arms to another.

At one point, Naomi stood by the kitchen doorway, watching the scene unfold—the hum of conversation, the soft glow of lamplight, the sound of her children giggling. Tears filled her eyes.

Christopher walked up beside her, sliding an arm around her waist. "Looks like the village showed up," he said quietly.

Naomi nodded. "God built this," she whispered. "Every single person in this room is part of His plan."

He smiled, his voice low and sure. "And I think He knew we'd need it. Love multiplied needs hands to hold it all."

Later that night, when the last guest left and the house finally grew quiet, Naomi slipped outside to the garden. The air was cool, the moon bright. She looked up and whispered, "Thank You, Lord. You didn't just give us a family. You surrounded us with one."

From somewhere deep within, she remembered the words from Ecclesiastes that Pastor Henry had once quoted: *Two are better than one...if either of them falls, one can help the other up.*

She smiled. *Two, three, or thirty—it's still true.*

That night, as she rocked one of the babies to sleep, Naomi felt an overwhelming peace. God had not only answered her prayer for help—He multiplied it. Through every act of kindness, He reminded her that His design for family was never meant to be isolated.

Love grew best in community. Strength multiplied in connection.

And as the triplets slept soundly in their cribs, Naomi realized that the same God who planted hope in her heart had also planted people around her—roots intertwined, strong and steady.

Chapter Seven

Provision in the Press

The joy of community had carried Naomi and Christopher through those early months, but as the triplets neared their first birthday, new pressures began to build. Bills arrived faster than paychecks, and the cost of diapers, formula, and doctor visits stacked like bricks on their shoulders.

Christopher had always been careful with money. He prided himself on providing, on making sure their home was secure. But lately, the math wasn't adding up. The agency had cut back on bonuses, and one of his side clients—who owed him months of payment—stopped returning calls altogether.

Each morning, he prayed for wisdom but worry still followed him to work like a shadow. He'd sit in his office, staring at spreadsheets, feeling the tug of anxiety coil tight in his chest.

Lord, I'm trying, he whispered one afternoon, hands clasped on the desk. *I'm doing all I can. But it's not enough.*

That's when he remembered a sermon Pastor Henry once preached: "Provision isn't about what you can produce—it's about what you're willing to trust God with." The words lingered, uncomfortable but true.

At home, Naomi felt the strain too. She could see it in Christopher's silence, the furrow of his brow, the long hours he spent on his laptop at night. She tried to help by cutting corners—shopping sales, cooking from scratch, even selling a few gently used baby clothes online—but the worry still crept in.

One evening, after the triplets were asleep, she found Christopher sitting on the couch, staring at the checkbook. The room was dim, lit only by the flicker of a lamp.

"Talk to me," she said softly, sitting beside him.

He rubbed his temples. "I'm just…trying to figure out how to stretch what we have. I don't want you to worry."

She touched his hand. "But I do worry, Chris. We're in this together. Maybe it's time we stop trying to carry it and start trusting God with it."

He looked at her, weary but moved. "You still believe He'll show up?"

She smiled faintly. "I don't just believe it. I've seen it. Every time I thought we were at the end of ourselves, grace found us. Why would this be any different?"

That week, Naomi began waking early—before dawn, before the babies stirred—to pray in the nursery. She would walk softly between the cribs, whispering Scriptures over their little lives.

"The Lord is my shepherd; I shall not want. My God shall supply all your need according to His riches in glory."

Each morning, she felt a quiet reassurance. It wasn't that their situation suddenly changed, but her perspective did. Peace took the place of panic.

And then, as often happens when faith takes root, provision began to bloom in unexpected places. It started with a letter.

One Thursday afternoon, Naomi checked the mail and found an envelope from an old employer—a company she'd worked for years before motherhood. Inside was a note explaining that the company had reviewed its retirement contributions and owed her a payout she had never claimed. It wasn't a fortune, but it was enough to cover their most pressing bills.

She called Christopher immediately. "You're not going to believe this," she said, voice trembling with excitement. "God just reminded us He sees us."

He laughed, a deep, relieved laugh she hadn't heard in months. "Provision in the press," he said. "That's exactly what this is."

The blessings didn't stop there. A week later, the church announced a new grant program for families in ministry. Pastor Henry nominated them without telling them, and when the committee approved it, they received a small monthly stipend to help with childcare. Then, out of nowhere, Christopher's overdue client reached out, apologizing profusely and transferring full payment—with a bonus for the delay.

Each time, they looked at one another in awe. It wasn't coincidence; it was confirmation. But perhaps the greatest shift wasn't financial—it was spiritual.

Naomi and Christopher began to see provision not as money or means, but as *God's presence meeting their need in every form.* Some days, it was a hot meal from a neighbor. Other days, it was a moment of laughter that eased the weight of worry.

One night, Christopher turned to Naomi as they sat watching the baby's sleep.

"You know," he said, "I used to think faith meant doing everything right so God would bless us. But now I think faith is believing He's blessing us even when everything looks wrong."

Naomi nodded, her heart full. "Exactly. It's not the size of the paycheck. It's the size of our peace."

Later that week, Christopher received an unexpected call from his supervisor.

"Chris, we've been reviewing leadership roles for the new quarter," his boss said. "Your consistency hasn't gone unnoticed. We'd like to promote you to senior consultant. It comes with a raise and the flexibility to work from home a few days a week."

He nearly dropped the phone. When he told Naomi, she threw her hands over her mouth, tears streaming down her cheeks.

"God, You did it again," she whispered. "You provided not just for our needs, but for our time together."

They both stood in the kitchen, holding each other amid the scent of dinner still simmering on the stove, the babies' laughter echoing down the hall.

That night, Naomi journaled as she always did when her heart overflowed:

When the pressure came, we feared the breaking—but God used it to press out faith instead of fear. Provision isn't about having everything we want. It's about realizing we already have everything we need when we seek Him first.

She paused, watching Christopher bounce one of the babies on his knee, singing softly. Peace settled around her like a familiar friend.

We were never meant to handle the press alone. Every squeeze was a setup for oil to flow—for anointing, for testimony, for trust.

As the night deepened, Naomi and Christopher stood by the window, the moonlight casting silver across the garden. Christopher slipped his arm around her waist.

"You know what I've learned?" he said.

"What's that?"

"That provision isn't the absence of pressure. It's the miracle that grows inside it."

Naomi leaned into him, smiling. "Then I guess we're standing in a miracle right now."

And they were. In the press, their faith had been refined. In the pressure, their peace had multiplied. And once again, grace had proven more than enough.

CHAPTER EIGHT

REDISCOVERING US

By the time the triplets turned one, life had begun to settle into something resembling rhythm. There were still late nights, still endless laundry, still moments when exhaustion pressed in, but there was laughter again. The house echoed with giggles and the patter of tiny hands slapping the floor as three curious explorers found their way into everything.

Yet somewhere between diaper changes and dinner time, between ministry calls and midnight feedings, Naomi realized she and Christopher hadn't really looked at each other in weeks. Not just *seen* each other, but *seen*.

Their conversations revolved around logistics, not life. Their laughter had become family laughter, not the quiet, shared kind that belonged only to them. And though love was present, intimacy had slipped quietly into the background, replaced by schedules and survival.

One evening, after the babies were asleep and the dishes were done, Naomi stood at the window, watching the moonlight fall over the garden. Christopher joined her, wrapping his arm loosely around her waist. They stood in silence, the kind that carried both comfort and distance.

"Do you ever miss us?" she asked softly.

He turned toward her, his brow furrowed. "Us?"

"The version of us before…all this." She motioned toward the nursery. "Before bottles, and burp cloths, and…exhaustion."

He exhaled slowly. "Yeah," he admitted, "I do. But I wouldn't trade what we have now for what we had then."

Naomi smiled faintly. "Neither would I. I just…miss knowing you beyond the noise."

The next day, Naomi found herself thinking about his words. *What did knowing him look like now?* She remembered their early days—coffee dates after church, evening walks where they dreamed aloud about the future, spontaneous prayer sessions that often ended in laughter and tears.

Somewhere between then and now, those moments had been replaced by routine. And though routine had its place, it had also dulled the spark that once burned so freely between them.

That afternoon, Naomi called her friend Denise.

"I need a favor," she said, smiling through the phone. "Can you watch the babies Friday night?"

Denise didn't even hesitate. "Absolutely. Are you two finally taking a night off?"

"Trying to," Naomi replied. "It's time."

Friday came, and for the first time in over a year, the house fell silent—no cries, no toys clattering, no bedtime chaos. Just quiet.

Naomi stood in front of the mirror, smoothing her dress. It wasn't fancy, but it made her feel like herself again. Christopher peeked into the room and froze, smiling.

"Wow," he said softly. "You look…beautiful."

Naomi blushed. "It's been a while since I've heard that."

"Well," he grinned, "it's been a while since I've had the chance to say it."

They went to a small café downtown; the kind of place that played soft jazz and served coffee in oversized mugs. At first, the conversation was awkward. They talked about the kids, the bills, church projects. But somewhere between the first sip of coffee and the shared dessert, something shifted.

Christopher leaned back, eyes warm. "Do you remember when we used to dream out loud?"

Naomi smiled. "How could I forget? You wanted to open a youth center, and I wanted to write a book about faith and motherhood."

He chuckled. "And here we are—leading youth retreats and living the book you wanted to write."

She laughed, realizing he was right. "We really are."

Then the laughter softened and the air between them changed. The spark that had gone quiet flickered again.

When they returned home, the house was still, the triplets sleeping soundly. Naomi walked into the nursery, brushed her fingers over each crib, and whispered a prayer of gratitude. Then she turned to find Christopher watching her from the doorway.

"You know," he said, his voice tender, "I think we forgot that our marriage is also part of God's ministry."

She nodded slowly. "We've been serving everyone else, but not each other."

"Exactly." He walked closer, taking her hand. "Maybe rediscovering us starts with remembering that love is worship too."

Over the next few weeks, they began rebuilding connection, one small gesture at a time.

Christopher started leaving her little notes—verses scribbled on scraps of paper tucked under her coffee mug or left on the bathroom mirror. Naomi, in turn, packed his lunch with handwritten prayers and encouraging quotes.

They started praying together again at night, not rushed prayers but heart prayers—the kind that invited laughter and tears. Sometimes, they'd turn off the TV, sit in silence, and simply talk. Other nights, they'd dance in the living room to soft worship songs, their laughter blending with the gentle hum of grace.

Slowly, intimacy returned; not just the physical closeness, but the emotional tenderness that had been buried beneath duty. They began to see each other as partners again, not just parents.

One evening, Christopher surprised her with a candlelit dinner in the backyard. String lights hung between the trees, casting a soft glow over the table. Naomi gasped, tears springing to her eyes.

"You did all this?"

He smiled. "You once said you missed knowing me beyond the noise. Well, here I am."

They sat for hours, talking about dreams, faith, and everything in between. Naomi felt herself exhale; not the tired kind, but the peaceful kind that comes when the heart remembers joy.

As the night drew to a close, Christopher reached across the table, his voice low. "You know what I think, Naomi?"

"What's that?"

"I think rediscovering us isn't about going back. It's about growing deeper, loving each other with the lessons we've learned, not the expectations we used to have."

Her eyes filled again. "Then I guess we're right where we're supposed to be."

That night, Naomi wrote in her journal:

Marriage, like faith, must be tended. Neglect is the fox that creeps in quietly, stealing joy little by little. But love—true love—chooses to rebuild, to forgive, to laugh again. Today, we caught the foxes and remembered that we are still a vineyard in bloom.

She closed the journal, feeling lighter than she had in months. Beside her, Christopher was already asleep, his hand resting over hers.

Naomi smiled. The journey wasn't perfect, but it was theirs—growing, blooming, rooted in grace.

And as she drifted into sleep, one thought lingered like a prayer: *When love is watered with grace, it doesn't just survive—it flourishes.*

Chapter Nine

The Power of Words

The house sounded different now. Not quieter; just softer. There was still laughter echoing down the hallways, still the occasional cry or tumble, still toys scattered across the living room floor like confetti from a celebration no one remembered ending. But beneath it all was a gentler rhythm, a steadiness that hadn't been there before.

Naomi noticed it one morning as she stood at the kitchen sink, rinsing bottles while sunlight spilled across the counter. The triplets were babbling in the next room, their voices rising and falling in an uncoordinated symphony. Christopher was humming softly as he packed lunches, the sound low and unassuming.

Nothing about their schedule had changed. Nothing about their responsibilities had lessened. And yet, the atmosphere felt lighter.

She paused, hands resting in the warm water, and realized the difference wasn't what they were doing; it was what they were saying.

There had been a time when exhaustion had shaped her language.

"I can't keep up."

"This is too much."

"I'm failing at this."

She hadn't meant harm by the words. They were honest. They were familiar. They felt justified. But honesty without hope had quietly begun shaping the walls of their home.

Now, without fully noticing when it started, her words had shifted.

"We're learning."

"God has been faithful again."

"Grace is meeting us today."

She wasn't pretending the days were easy. She was choosing not to let her words partner with fear in spaces God had already filled with grace.

Naomi dried her hands and leaned against the counter, watching Christopher move through the kitchen. She realized something that startled her with its simplicity: Words didn't just describe their days. They directed them.

Later that afternoon, Christopher sat on the floor with the triplets, stacking blocks that were immediately knocked down by eager hands. One child clapped at the collapse, another laughed, the third attempted to eat a block.

"Well," Christopher chuckled, "that's one way to redesign architecture."

Naomi smiled from the doorway. There was a time when moments like this would have ended in frustration—sharp words spoken too quickly, silence lingering too long. Now, even the mistakes felt lighter.

That evening, after the children were asleep and the house had settled into its familiar quiet, Naomi brought up what had been stirring in her heart.

"Have you noticed," she asked gently, "how different things feel lately?"

Christopher leaned back against the couch, thoughtful. "I have. I just couldn't put my finger on why."

"I think it's our words," she said. "Not just what we say to each other, but what we say about our lives."

He nodded slowly. "I've been thinking about that too. I realized something the other day at work."

She turned toward him.

"I used to come home and talk about pressure—deadlines, expectations, responsibilities. And none of it was untrue. But I started noticing how heavy the house felt afterward. Like I'd brought the weight in with me."

"So, what changed?" she asked.

"I stopped leading with frustration," he said quietly. "Not because it disappeared, but because I didn't want it to be the loudest voice in our home. Our family doesn't need me to have everything figured out. They need me to speak faith when things are uncertain."

Naomi felt the truth of his words settle deep inside her. Leadership wasn't always loud. Sometimes, it sounded like peace spoken deliberately.

The real test came a few days later.

The morning unraveled quickly—a missed appointment, a spilled cup of juice, a bill that arrived unexpectedly in the mail. Naomi felt the familiar tension rise in her chest. Old words pressed against her lips, ready and rehearsed.

"This is too much."

She stopped herself.

The children were watching; not because they understood the situation, but because they always listened.

She took a breath and said instead, "Okay. This is hard. But we're going to handle it together."

The moment passed quietly, but something shifted. The air felt steadier. Her heart did too.

That night, Naomi and Christopher prayed aloud together. Not rushed prayers spoken out of habit, but intentional ones. They thanked God *out loud*. They named His faithfulness *out loud*. They declared peace over their home *out loud*.

Naomi realized something then: faith spoken consistently carried more weight than fear spoken impulsively.

The triplets, now learning their first words, became living reminders of the power of language. Naomi watched them carefully—how they mimicked tone before meaning, how they repeated sounds they heard often. They were learning how to speak. And without realizing it, they were also learning how to believe.

One afternoon, as Naomi sat journaling, she wrote:

I used to think words were reactions. I know now they are invitations. What I speak welcomes something into my home—fear or faith, weariness or worship. Grace multiplied when I stopped asking God to change my circumstances and started allowing Him to change my language.

She closed the journal slowly, feeling the weight—and freedom—of that truth. Words had shaped her waiting. Words had softened her abundance. Words were now preparing her testimony.

That evening, as Christopher tucked the children into bed, he whispered over them, "You are loved. You are safe. God is with you."

Naomi stood in the doorway, listening. This, she realized, was how grace multiplied—not always through miracles shouted from rooftops, but through faith spoken daily, quietly, faithfully.

The house grew still. And once again, grace had filled the space where fear used to live.

CHAPTER TEN

FAITH IN THE SMALL MOMENTS

Morning light spilled softly across the nursery floor, dancing between the wooden bars of the cribs. Naomi stood quietly in the doorway, her heart swelling at the sight before her—three tiny miracles, once fragile and new, now chattering to one another in baby babble that sounded like laughter wrapped in sunlight.

Every morning felt sacred now. The chaos hadn't disappeared—the triplets still woke at odd hours and laundry still formed mountains—but Naomi's heart had changed. The things that once felt small, even insignificant, now shimmered with holy purpose.

She'd begun to see God in the rhythm of it all. In the way Christopher's laughter filled the house, in the squeak of the rocking chair as she prayed over the babies, even in the quiet moments between chores when gratitude welled up unexpectedly.

Each act of care had become an altar. It happened gradually—this awareness that God was near in the ordinary.

One afternoon, while folding tiny socks, Naomi realized she was humming. The tune wasn't familiar, but it felt comforting, like worship woven into routine.

She smiled and whispered, "Even this, Lord—this folding, this serving, this stillness—it's for You."

Later that day, she found herself sitting on the porch, watching the triplets play on a blanket in the yard. Their garden was in full bloom again. The flowers waved gently in the breeze, a living reminder of where their journey had begun. She thought of all the nights she'd prayed for miracles, never realizing that the miracle was already here, growing right in front of her, one ordinary day at a time.

When Christopher came home that evening, she met him at the door with a soft smile.

"You seem peaceful," he said, setting down his bag.

"I think I am," she replied. "I'm learning that faith isn't just about trusting God in the big moments. It's about seeing Him in the small ones too."

He looked around the house—toys scattered, dishes drying on the rack, one of the babies trying to crawl after a stray spoon.

"You mean in this beautiful mess?"

Naomi laughed. "Exactly."

He nodded slowly. "Then we're right where we're supposed to be."

That night, after dinner, they sat together at the kitchen table. Christopher was feeding Peace and Naomi was trying to spoon mashed sweet potato into Boldness, who found more joy in flinging it than eating it. Compassion, meanwhile, was babbling a conversation with her reflection in the highchair tray.

Christopher laughed. "You ever feel like we're running a small circus?"

"Every day," Naomi replied, giggling. "But I think God's the ringmaster."

Their laughter filled the room, light and sincere. And in that laughter, Naomi felt something sacred—a joy that didn't depend on perfection, only on presence.

Later, after the triplets were tucked in, Naomi and Christopher sat quietly on the couch. The house was finally still; the kind of stillness that made you exhale deeply.

Naomi looked at him. "Remember when everything felt too hard to handle?"

He nodded. "I do."

"Now look at us," she said softly. "Still tired, still learning, but still standing."

Christopher smiled, resting his head back. "It's the small things that kept us, Naomi. The prayers whispered half-asleep, the forgiveness after long days, the smiles we didn't feel like giving but gave anyway."

Naomi reached for his hand. "Those were the moments that built our faith."

That weekend, she decided to start something new—a gratitude journal. Not the kind that waited for big blessings, but one that celebrated the everyday grace that made life sacred. Her first entry read:

Today, I saw God in the sunlight pouring over our kitchen table. I saw Him in Christopher's patience, in the giggle of our babies, in the warmth of our home. I used to wait for miracles. Now, I realize, I wake up in them every day.

She added a small drawing of three tiny footprints below the words, then smiled to herself.

A few days later, Christopher found the journal open on the counter. He skimmed her words and chuckled.

"You even wrote about my patience?"

Naomi grinned. "Don't ruin the moment."

He kissed her forehead. "You're teaching me something, you know. I'm always waiting for the next big thing, but maybe faith is learning to love the in-between."

She looked up at him, her eyes soft. "That's where God grows us the most."

That evening, as the triplets played in their playpen, Naomi picked up her guitar—an old, dusty thing she hadn't touched in years. She began strumming softly, humming a simple melody. The babies turned their heads toward her, curious. Christopher peeked from the doorway, smiling.

"I didn't know you still played," he said.

"I forgot I did," she answered. "Guess I'm remembering now."

She began to sing a simple refrain that came straight from her heart:

"In the little things, You're faithful. In the quiet, You are near. In the waiting and the working, Your presence is right here."

Her voice trembled, but it was pure. When she finished, Christopher clapped softly.

"That's beautiful."

Naomi smiled. "It's not just a song. It's a reminder."

Later that night, she wrote her final journal entry for the day:

Faith isn't built in the spotlight; it's nurtured in the shadows. It's not measured by size, but by sincerity. Every diaper change, every prayer, every shared laugh, they're all sacred if done with love. Maybe the small moments aren't small at all.

She closed the journal and looked around the room—the soft glow of the lamp, the hum of the monitor, the rhythmic breathing of her family asleep nearby.

Naomi whispered into the quiet, "Thank You, Lord, for meeting me here, in the small, in the ordinary, in the now."

And as peace settled over the house like a blanket, she realized the truth that had been growing quietly in her spirit all along: *God doesn't just move in miracles. He dwells in the moments we choose to see Him.*

Part III:

When Grace Multiplies

From personal miracle to living testimony.

CHAPTER ELEVEN

GRACE MULTIPLIED

The sanctuary buzzed with quiet anticipation that Sunday morning. Naomi could feel the hum of expectancy ripple through the pews as families greeted one another, children laughed, and the worship team prepared to play. She sat near the front with Christopher and the triplets—their once-tiny babies now toddling, babbling, and testing the limits of patience and pew space.

It had been two years since that unexpected phone call from the agency, and sometimes, Naomi still woke up astonished at how God had rewritten their story. What once was silence and waiting had become a symphony of joy and noise.

When Pastor Henry stepped to the pulpit, he smiled knowingly. "Church, today we get to hear a testimony that reminds us how God multiplies His grace when we surrender our plans for His."

Naomi felt her stomach flutter. She'd prayed for

the right words all week, but as she stood, holding Christopher's hand, she realized something simple. This testimony wasn't really about *her words*. It was about *His faithfulness*.

They walked together to the front, the congregation leaning forward with love. Naomi glanced at Christopher, who gave her a small nod.

"I used to think grace was something you received when you failed," she began, her voice trembling slightly. "But now I know it's also what sustains you when you succeed; when blessings come faster than your strength can handle."

The room grew quiet.

"When God blessed us with our three little miracles," she continued, smiling toward the toddlers now waving to the congregation, "I thought I needed to be perfect—the perfect mother, the perfect wife, the perfect believer. But God gently reminded me, again and again, that His grace isn't earned through perfection. It meets us in our weakness, multiplies in our chaos, and strengthens us in our surrender."

A soft murmur of amen rippled through the church.

Christopher stepped forward next, his voice steady but full of emotion. "When we first brought the triplets home, I thought my job was to hold everything together—financially, emotionally, spiritually. But I learned that faith doesn't mean holding tight. It means letting go. It means trusting that God's provision doesn't stop when pressure comes. He provides in the press."

He paused, glancing at Naomi with a small smile.

"I watched my wife find peace in the middle of exhaustion and that peace began to change our home. Grace taught us how to laugh again, how to rest again, how to love again. And now, standing here, I realize grace didn't just carry us. It multiplied us."

Applause filled the sanctuary. Tears shimmered in the eyes of several parents who had prayed their own long prayers for children, for peace, for hope.

Naomi felt her heart swell. She thought of every sleepless night, every whispered prayer, every moment she thought she wasn't enough. And then, she looked at the faces before her—friends, church members, even strangers—and realized something profound: *their story was no longer just theirs.*

Grace, when shared, multiplies.

After the service, people lined up to hug them, thank them, and whisper their own stories of waiting, believing, and holding on.

An older woman squeezed Naomi's hand and said, "You reminded me that it's never too late for God to move."

A young couple with tears in their eyes said, "We were ready to give up on adoption, but your story gave us hope again."

Each encounter was a seed of faith sown into someone else's soil.

As Naomi and Christopher packed up the kids to go home, Christopher turned to her with a grin.

"I think today wasn't just about us telling our story. It was about reminding everyone that God's still writing theirs."

Naomi smiled, her heart light. "Exactly. Grace multiplies when it's shared."

That afternoon, after the children's nap time, Naomi found herself sitting in the garden—the same patch of earth that had witnessed every season of their journey. The flowers were taller now, vibrant and strong. She traced her fingers along the petals and whispered, "You've seen it all, haven't you?"

The wind rustled softly, as if nodding in agreement.

She opened her journal, the pages now worn and full—prayers, lessons, small miracles, moments of surrender. Slowly, she began to write:

Grace doesn't just restore what was lost. It multiplies what was planted. One act of faith becomes a harvest of testimony. One moment of surrender becomes a story that reaches hearts we'll never meet.

She looked up as Christopher stepped outside, holding one of the toddlers who was clutching a toy in each hand.

"Writing again?" he asked with a grin.

"Always," she said, closing the journal softly. "It's how I keep track of grace."

That evening, their home was filled with music and laughter. Christopher turned on one of their favorite gospel playlists and the triplets were dancing—or rather, wobbling joyfully—across the living room floor. Naomi clapped along, tears of joy slipping down her cheeks.

In the middle of the laughter, Christopher caught her hand, spinning her gently into an impromptu dance. The toddlers squealed with delight, joining in their uncoordinated rhythm.

"This," Naomi said breathlessly, laughing as she twirled, "is what grace looks like."

Christopher nodded, his eyes warm. "Messy, joyful, and multiplied."

They laughed again, the music rising, the house alive with light.

Later, after bedtime stories and lullabies, Naomi whispered the same blessing she always did. "You are loved. You are covered. You are chosen."

As she closed the nursery door, she paused—not to listen for cries, but to listen to the quiet hum of peace that filled their home. In that stillness, she felt the Holy Spirit whisper back: *My grace will keep multiplying.*

Naomi returned to the living room, where Christopher was waiting with two cups of tea. They sat together in the glow of lamplight, hands intertwined, hearts full.

"Do you ever wonder what's next?" she asked softly.

He smiled. "Whatever it is, we'll face it the same way we faced everything else—with grace."

Naomi nodded, resting her head on his shoulder. "Grace upon grace."

The room fell quiet again, the kind of quiet that feels like a prayer. Outside, the wind moved gently through the garden, rustling the flowers where hope first took root.

Chapter Twelve

Blessed Beyond Measure

The garden was quiet that morning, the kind of stillness that seemed to hum with gratitude. Naomi stood among the flowers, the dew clinging to her sandals as the early sunlight poured across the earth. She could hear the soft sound of the triplets' laughter drifting from the house—a melody sweeter than any song.

It had been three years since that miraculous call that changed everything. The whirlwind of baby bottles and sleepless nights had given way to playful mornings, toddler chaos, and bedtime prayers whispered in triplicate. The days were still full—sometimes too full—but there was peace in the fullness now.

Naomi bent down to touch the soil, her fingers tracing the same patch she once cried over—the place where she'd asked God for a new beginning. Now, it was bursting with color. Roses, lilies, daisies—each one a living reminder that what begins in faith always ends in fruitfulness.

Behind her, Christopher's voice broke through the morning air. "They escaped again!"

Naomi turned to see him jogging toward her, three little pairs of feet pattering beside him, each child clutching something they probably shouldn't have—a toy truck, a wooden spoon, and a fistful of flowers freshly plucked from the garden.

She laughed, shaking her head. "You can't outrun blessings," she teased.

"Or contain them," he said, catching his breath.

Naomi knelt down as the triplets barreled toward her. She hugged them close, the scent of their shampoo and sunlight filling her senses.

"You three are my miracle harvest," she whispered.

Later that day, as the family gathered for lunch, the house buzzed with familiar noise—laughter, clinking dishes, and the occasional "Don't put that in your mouth!" Christopher set the table while Naomi carried in plates of food. It was simple, nothing fancy, but the joy at that table was abundance itself.

Christopher raised his glass of lemonade and smiled. "To grace multiplied," he said.

Naomi nodded, her eyes soft. "And to the God who multiplies it."

They clinked glasses, the triplets giggling and trying to copy them, lemonade sloshing everywhere.

"Blessed beyond measure," Christopher said quietly, meeting her gaze.

Naomi smiled. "Beyond anything we could have asked or imagined."

That afternoon, while the children napped, Naomi sat at her desk by the window. She opened her journal, now filled with years of prayers, reflections, and tiny scribbles from toddler hands. She began to write her final entry:

We started this journey praying for one blessing and God gave us three. But the true miracle wasn't just what He placed in our arms. It was what He formed in our hearts. Grace taught us how to surrender, faith taught us how to see, and love taught us how to stay. We've been stretched, refined, and renewed, and through it all, God has remained constant. This home is living proof that when we sow with tears, we truly do reap with songs of joy.

She paused, the words settling like peace in her spirit.

In the backyard, Christopher was playing with the children; three tiny whirlwinds chasing him around the garden. Naomi watched from the porch, her heart overflowing.

The sound of their laughter filled the air—wild, unfiltered, and full of life. It struck her that blessing didn't always look neat or polished. Sometimes, it was loud, messy, and bursting with movement. But it was still holy.

She whispered a quiet prayer. "Lord, thank You. You turned our waiting into wonder and our tears into testimony."

As if on cue, a soft breeze brushed her cheek, carrying the faint scent of lilies; the same kind that had bloomed the day she first prayed here.

That evening, as the sun dipped low and painted the sky in streaks of pink and gold, Naomi and Christopher sat together on the porch steps, the triplets playing in the yard. Christopher leaned back, watching them.

"You ever think about how far we've come?"

Naomi nodded. "Every day. Sometimes, I still can't believe it."

He smiled. "Remember that first night—the chaos, the bottles, the exhaustion?"

"How could I forget?" she laughed. "We were drowning in diapers."

"And now look at us," he said, gesturing toward the children. "Still tired. Still learning. But blessed beyond measure."

Naomi rested her head on his shoulder. "It wasn't an easy blessing," she whispered. "But it was a perfect one."

He squeezed her hand. "Because it came through grace."

They sat quietly for a long time, the soft chirp of crickets filling the air, the children's laughter fading into the sounds of evening.

Later that night, after the house had grown still, Naomi walked into the nursery one last time. The moonlight fell gently across the room, casting silver patterns on the floor.

She whispered her nightly blessing; the same one she had spoken since their first week home. "You are loved. You are covered. You are chosen." Then she added softly, "And you are proof that God's promises never return void."

She stood there for a moment, letting the truth of it settle deep in her heart. Every struggle, every tear, every prayer had led to this—a home overflowing with joy, anchored in grace.

Before heading to bed, Naomi stepped out onto the porch. The night air was cool; the stars scattered like whispers of glory across the sky. She closed her eyes and breathed deeply.

This, she thought, *is what it means to be blessed beyond measure.*

It wasn't about having everything she wanted. It was about knowing the One who had given her everything she needed—peace in the storm, strength in the press, laughter in the chaos, and love that multiplied again and again.

As she turned to go inside, she saw Christopher standing at the doorway, watching her with a gentle smile.

"What are you thinking about?" he asked.

Naomi smiled back, her eyes shining. "Just that I finally understand what grace upon grace looks like."

He reached for her hand. "And?"

"And" she said, squeezing his fingers, "it looks a lot like this."

Together, they walked inside, hand in hand, their home glowing softly behind them—a beacon of faith, love, and promise fulfilled.

And in the stillness that followed, the sound of the triplets' quiet breathing became its own kind of hymn—a lullaby of grace, a melody of joy, a reminder that hope, once planted, always grows.

When God multiplies grace, He doesn't just restore what was lost—He builds something new from the ashes, something rooted in faith, watered by love, and blooming in hope. Blessed beyond measure isn't a season; it's a testimony; one that keeps growing wherever His presence is planted.

When this journey began, Naomi and Christopher were two people learning how to trust God through waiting, heartbreak, and hope. By the time we leave them here, with laughter echoing through their home and the garden blooming again, their story has become something bigger: a testimony that God's grace multiplies when we least expect it.

Grace is not neat or predictable. It rarely arrives according to our timetable or wrapped in the package we imagined. Sometimes, it comes as a whisper in the chaos. Sometimes, it walks through the door carrying more than we asked for. And often, it looks like love that refuses to quit.

Through every season—the stillness of waiting, the stretch of obedience, the press of provision, and the joy of rediscovery—we've watched Naomi and Christopher learn what it means to live anchored in faith. They learned that grace doesn't just visit the extraordinary moments; it inhabits the ordinary ones. It lingers in the sound of a baby's laughter, the quiet prayers between husband and wife, the helping hands of a village, and the garden where tears once fell but hope now grows.

They began their story praying for a single blessing. God answered with more than enough. He gave them triplets—symbols of His triune presence and multiplied favor. But, more importantly, He gave them new hearts. Hearts that understood that true blessing isn't measured by numbers or noise, but by presence—His presence, constant and sure.

Where Hope Took Root
Grace Multiplied

36 Discussion Questions
& Prayer

CHAPTER 1 — THE UNEXPECTED CALL

1. How does Naomi and Christopher's reaction to the agency's call reveal the tension between desire and readiness?
2. What does this chapter teach us about God giving more than we ask for?
3. Have you ever received a blessing that felt bigger than your capacity? How did you navigate it?

CHAPTER 2 — OVERFLOWING EMOTIONS

4. Where do you see God meeting Naomi and Christopher in the chaos of early parenthood?
5. Why do you think grace is often easiest to recognize in hindsight rather than in real time?
6. What "messy moments" in your life have become evidence of God's presence?

CHAPTER 3 — LEARNING TO BREATHE AGAIN

7. Why do blessings sometimes feel like burdens at first?
8. How do you handle seasons when God stretches you beyond your comfort zone?
9. What does surrender look like when you're overwhelmed by goodness rather than hardship?

CHAPTER 4 —TRINITY IN THE CRIB

10. What do the babies' individual personalities teach Naomi and Christopher about God's nature?
11. Have you ever experienced God revealing Himself through everyday life?
12. How does dedicating the children symbolize deeper spiritual surrender?

CHAPTER 5 — WHEN LOVE FEELS THIN

13. Why is it easy for relationships to suffer during seasons of responsibility?
14. What can this chapter teach us about loving through exhaustion?
15. How does God use emotional distance to invite reconnection?

CHAPTER 6 — THE VILLAGE GOD BUILT

16. Why is community essential in seasons of blessing?
17. How does pride sometimes keep us from receiving help?
18. Who has been part of your "village," and how have they carried you?

Chapter 7 — Provision in the Press

19. How does this chapter redefine what provision looks like?
20. What happens when we trust God with our lack instead of trying to fix it alone?
21. Can you recognize moments when God provided in unexpected ways?

Chapter 8 — Rediscovering Us

22. Why is intentional connection necessary for healthy relationships?
23. Which spiritual practices help couples rediscover one another during demanding seasons?
24. How can we protect emotional intimacy while managing heavy responsibilities?

Chapter 9 — The Power of Words

25. What role do words play in shaping the atmosphere of a home?
26. How do Naomi and Christopher's spoken declarations shift their daily experiences?
27. What declarations do you need to begin speaking over your own life?

CHAPTER 10 — FAITH IN THE SMALL MOMENTS

28. How does Naomi learn to recognize God in small routines and ordinary tasks?

29. Why is faith built more through consistency than dramatic moments?

30. Which small moments in your life reveal God's presence most clearly?

CHAPTER 11 — GRACE MULTIPLIED

31. Why is it powerful to share testimonies publicly?

32. What does this chapter show about how grace grows when it's shared?

33. How has God multiplied grace in your own story?

CHAPTER 12 — BLESSED BEYOND MEASURE

34. How does Naomi's journey show that blessing requires stewardship as much as gratitude?

35. Why is it important to look back and acknowledge what God has done?

36. What part of your story do you now see as "blessed beyond measure," even if it didn't feel like it at first?

A Prayer of Strength, Surrender, and Sustaining Grace

Lord, Thank You for every moment of grace You have poured into my life—the grace that met me in waiting, the grace that held me in weakness, and the grace that carried me when blessings felt bigger than my strength.

As this journey ends, I ask that You continue to multiply Your presence in my life. Teach me to see You in the chaos, to trust You in the stretching, and to lean on You in the moments that feel heavy.

Give me the courage to embrace abundance without fear and the wisdom to rest in Your sufficiency. Strengthen my heart to love well, serve faithfully, and walk confidently in the purpose You have written for me.

May Your joy be my strength, Your peace be my anchor, Your Word be my guide, and Your grace be my daily portion.

Let every blessing in my life reflect Your goodness. Let every challenge reveal Your faithfulness. Let every day be a reminder that I am upheld by grace upon grace. Amen.

ABOUT THE AUTHOR

Dr. Annette West is a powerhouse of purpose, faith, and global influence. She holds a **Doctorate in Business Administration, Doctorate in Pastoral Counseling** and **Master's in Management Science**, blending marketplace wisdom with spiritual insight to empower women on their journey toward financial confidence and divine alignment.

She owns a prolific book publishing company. As a purpose-driven entity, JATNE Publishing exists to amplify voices. The company is dedicated to producing works that inspire transformation, champion Kingdom values, and equip readers to live boldly in their calling. Through professional guidance, creative excellence, and a heart for ministry, they partner with authors to bring meaningful, mission-centered messages to life.

As a book author, Dr. West has written numerous books designed to inspire readers to deepen their faith, embrace their God-given calling, and boldly build lives and businesses rooted in kingdom principles. This is now the beginning of her journey into Christian Fiction.

She is the voice of **Livingword International Ministry**, passionately serving as a dedicated **Servant Leader**, **Bible teacher**, **missionary**, and **media personality**, committed to spreading the gospel around the world. Her mission work has impacted lives across **Sierra Leone**, **Nigeria**, **Nairobi**, **Kakamega**, **Kenya**, and **India** where she continues to sow seeds of hope, healing, and transformation.

She is the founder of **Sisters of Valor**, a dynamic women's ministry committed to equipping and encouraging women to rise in their God-given identity and walk boldly in purpose. Dr. West also brings bold voices to the forefront through her **weekly podcast, "Dr. Annette Publishing Pusher"** on **Positive Power XXI Media**, where she interviews authors and entrepreneurs with stories that inspire and uplift. Also, the Talking All Things Books weekly session where all things related to books are shared.

Her influence expands into television through her powerful faith-based show on **Dekalb25.com**,

"**Livingword International Outreach Ministry,**" where she engages audiences in topics of spiritual growth and purposeful living.

Whether empowering book authors, preaching the Word, mentoring women, hosting global broadcasts, or planting seeds across nations, Dr. Annette West is a woman on a mission—pushing purpose, publishing, and prosperity forward for the glory of God.

DEVOTIONAL PROJECT INVITE

If you want to be part of a collaboration, join our next Centered in Christ devotional project. Each devotional project will have a particular theme. Each publication will be written and published to help readers gain a more robust understanding of Scriptures and learn ways of life application through reading stories of contributing authors.

There is an opportunity for aspiring or seasoned book authors to join the JATNE team of contributing authors. You will be able to add your co- authored book to your shelf or another book to your marketing toolbox.

If interested, reach out to us at Jatnepublishing.org

WRITE – WRITER – WRITING

If you are ready to pull thought from your mind and get it on paper, JATNE Publishing is here to assist you in getting your message out. We work with Christian, Christian-fiction, faith-based, inspirational writers, poets, and business professionals who are eager to publish books with information and life application to build their audience.

Join one of our workshops or programs:

- Jumpstart Your Writing Workshop: Gain foundational tools to get started with the writing process.
- Self-Publishing Boot Camp "SPBC": We guide you to write, publish, and launch your book in six months.
- Join Talking All Things Books: Weekly meetup, with the ability to ask a myriad of questions.

Contact JATNEpublishing.org

It's all about Faith–Family–Flourish, to move to the next level!

Other Faith Based Books by Dr. Annette West

Kingdom Promises The Beatitudes (2026)

Where Hope Took Root: Love, Loss and God Planted Something New (2025)

Centered in Christ, Developing My Identity and Self-Worth, Devotional, Vol V (2025)

Easy Indoor Gardening, Growing Vegetables and Herbs to Sustain Your Family (2024)

Centered in Christ, Praise Power Prayer in Worship Devotional, Vol IV (2024)

Centered in Christ, Life Him Up! Devotional, Vol III (2023)

Centered in Christ, Pursuing Peace, Vol II, (2022)

Centered in Christ, Steadfast and Immovable, Vol I (2021)

Marriage Connection Making It Work (2021)

Centered in Christ Anthology (2020)

Holistic Wellness Mind Body Spirit (2019)

Holistic Wellness Mind Body Spirit (Journal) (2019)

23-Day Devotional: The Book of Isaiah (2018)

Jesus, the Path to Victorious Living (2017)

Living Words of Encouragement Vol 2 (2016)

Living Words of Encouragement Vol 1 (2006)

Leadership Like Jesus (2003)

Basic Biblical Building Blocks (2002)

www.ingramcontent.com/pod-product-compliance
Lightning Source LLC
LaVergne TN
LVHW011047110826
845149LV00015B/3390

* 9 7 8 1 9 5 8 1 1 7 3 8 5 *